THIS BOOK BELONGS TO

....

To my three little piglets
Leonie, Henrietta and Maddox.
G.P.

Editor Jane O'Shea
Art editor Alison Fenton
Assisted by Hazel Bennington
and Alison Barclay
Production Jill Macey

First published in 1993 by
Conran Octopus Limited
37 Shelton Street, London WC2H 9HN

ISBN 1 85029 418 6

Imagesetting by Cymbol, London
Colour reproduction by Reed Reprographics, Suffolk
Printed and bound in Singapore

FRANK MUIR

RETELLS

THE THREE
LITTLE PIGS

THE HUMOROUS STORY OF A PIGLET ...
ANOTHER PIGLET ... AND YET ANOTHER PIGLET

Illustrated by Graham Philpot

CONRAN OCTOPUS

ONCE UPON A TIME (not very long ago) there were three little pigs.

Their mother was hopeless at thinking up names so because they were born on Good Friday she called them Hot, Cross and Bun.

Hot and Cross were boy piglets. Hot was always picking quarrels and not bothering to think much, while Cross was very bad-tempered and complained about everything. Cross did not think much, either, because he was usually too busy being bad-tempered.

Bun was a girl. She was shaped rather like a bun – comfortably round – and she was never – well, hardly ever – either quarrelsome or bad-tempered. She looked after her brothers without letting them know that she was looking after them. And Bun *did* think. She was really *good* at thinking.

Hot,

Cross,

and

Bun

It all started when a famous pop group played at the local theatre and smashed up their instruments as their grand finale. The three little pigs found the mess of broken guitars and drums in a skip and led by Bun they picked the bits out of the skip, took them home, glued them together and started their own pop group.

None of the piglets could play an instrument so they needed lots and lots of practice and they spent every day rehearsing in their bedroom. The noise they made was ear-splitting.

'I CAN'T STAND IT ANY LONGER!!!' their mother screamed at them one day (she had rammed apple cores into her ears but the noise was still dreadful). 'You'll have to go off and practise somewhere else!' she said. 'All the neighbours are complaining! The ginger cat next door has left home for good and a framed photograph of Mrs Bunny's granddad in his Fire-Brigade helmet fell off the wall and smashed. Build yourselves a rehearsal room deep in the forest. *Then* you can make as much noise as you like!'

So off into the forest trotted the three little pigs, clutching their glued-together guitars and drum kit.

They found a clearing and decided to have a quick practice.

'Twang! TWANG!' went Hot and Cross on their guitars.

'Boom! THUMP!!' went Bun on the drums. The piglets were busy rehearsing their first, indeed their only, song. It was a sad song.

'TWANG-G-G-G-!' went Hot, hitting a melancholy but loud note.

TWANG

'Twang-twang-TWANGGGGG-GGGGG!!' went Cross, with a flour-ish that produced a sound even sad-der and twice as loud.

'Boompity-boompity-**BOOM-BOOM-BOOM!!!**' went Bun, quite carried away, banging her drum with all her might.

In the trees and bushes a crowd of assorted woodland dwellers were gathering in fright, their voices almost drowned by the noise that Hot, Cross and Bun were making.

GGGGG!!!

'Call that music?' hooted a rather moth-eaten old owl. 'Who are they? What are they doing here?'

'I retired here for a bit of peace and quiet,' grumbled an elderly badger, his coat sticking up in protest like an old scrubbing brush. 'Somebody tell them to go!'

'I shall complain to Her Majesty the Queen of England and the Isle of Wight!' shrilled a small, unidentified bird who was a bit silly at the best of times.

'What a weally *fwightful* noise!' wailed a large, furry animal who was almost in tears about it.

The tearful animal was the Big Bad Wolf.

'I can't bear loud noises!' whimpered B.B. Wolf. 'I twied jamming cold sausages in my ears but that didn't help at *all*. And now I've got nothing to eat for supper!' A big tear rolled down the Wolf's cheek and he blew his nose loudly.

In fact 'B.B.' no longer stood for 'Big Bad'. The old wolf was so kind that the other animals voted him Furry Friend of the Year and he baby-sat for them (except for Thursday evenings when he had his cake-icing class). And he spent so much of the day snoozing on his big stuffed cushion that they changed his name to 'the Bean Bag Wolf'.

'TWANG! THUMP! VROOM!...' went the group.

'I'll tell you how to get rid of them,' said a quiet voice and all the animals went respectfully silent. They always did when the Brown Burmese Cat spoke because the Brown Burmese Cat was on holiday from being Resident Cat at Cheltenham High School for Girls and was highly intelligent. You could tell that because she was cleverly wearing a teacosy over her ears to muffle the piglets' horrible noise. It was a pretty pink tea-cosy embroidered in sequins with the message: 'Gang Easy Wi' the Tea-leaves, d'ye Ken?'.

'Wolf! You must *frighten* the little pigs away,' commanded the cat.

'Me? I couldn't fwighten a spoonful of yoghurt.'

'Then practise pulling ugly faces in the mirror. Puff out your chest. Try growling hideously instead of bleating like a goat.'

Stung into action, the Bean Bag Wolf went home and rehearsed being ugly and frightening. He became so good at pulling faces in the mirror that he frightened himself and had to sit down and have a comforting mug of warm milk.

Meanwhile Bun had decided that the little pigs should build themselves a rehearsal room in the woodland clearing.

'Ridiculous!' shouted Cross, red in the chaps with temper. 'Why build? We can practise in the open air and sleep in the bushes.'

'We need a rehearsal room so that our playing will not disturb the animals who live here,' explained Bun. 'Also it might rain and melt the glue on our guitars.'

'We can build our house from straw,' said Hot. 'That's quickest!'

'Oh, no, it must be stronger than that!' said Bun.

'Nonsense! Straw will do fine. Come on everybody!'

The little pigs scampered about collecting straw.

From the undergrowth the forest animals watched anxiously. When the hut was finished, the Brown Burmese Cat stepped forward, removed her pretty pink teacosy (it was giving her earache) and summoned B.B.Wolf.

'Try and frighten them away,' she commanded. 'If they won't go, blow their silly little straw house down.'

The B.B.Wolf crept up to the window, peered in, pulled his best nasty face and growled hideously.

The little pigs were tuning their instruments and not looking at the window so they missed the Wolf's performance.

'This is your tewwifying enemy, Wolf, bellowing!' bellowed the Bean Bag Wolf through the window in his best nasty voice. 'Leave the fowest at once or I'll huff and I'll puff and I'll *blow* your house down!'

But the piglets had begun playing again and did not hear him.

B.B.Wolf huffed and he puffed and he blew with all his might. (He then came over faint and had to have a sit-down.)

And...w h o o o s h ! . . . .

The straw house blew to the ground.

Bun was the first to emerge from the pile of straw which was all that was left. 'I told you,' she said to Hot. 'The weather's too windy for straw houses.'

'Straw was a stupid idea!' cried Cross angrily. 'Let's rebuild straight away with twigs. Plenty of twigs about.'

'I don't think twigs will be any better than straw,' Bun said.

'Of course they will, silly,' said her brother. 'Think of birds' nests! *They* don't blow down!'

So the three little pigs gathered twigs and built their new rehearsal room.

The woodland animals all watched. When the building was finished, the Brown Burmese Cat beckoned to the Bean Bag Wolf.

'Try to frighten them off,' she commanded. 'If they won't go, blow their silly twig house down.'

The Wolf glared in through the window of the twig house, making his second most frightful face.

'This is your tewwifying enemy, Wolf,' he bawled, 'saying "Hello again, little piglets!" I am here to warn you that if you do not leave the fowest immediately, I'll huff and I'll puff and I'll *blow* your twig house down!'

The little pigs took no notice because they were practising and they neither saw the Wolf making nasty faces at the window nor heard him shouting at them.

So the B.B. Wolf huffed and he puffed and... whoooosh!... he blew the little twig house down.

Bun was the first to crawl out of the pile of twigs that was the remains of their twiglet house.

'That does it!' she cried. 'This time we will do the job properly and build our house in *brick!* And I want no argument!'

Hot and Cross did not argue. They picked out the twigs which had lodged in their bristles and meekly followed Bun to a ruined hut in the woods where there were lots of old bricks lying about.

The woodland animals watched anxiously from the undergrowth as the three little pigs built up layer upon layer of bricks, and a strong building took shape. When it was almost finished, the piglets added a little chimney so that they could use a gasfire in cold weather. Then they began practising their music again.

'Wolf!' commanded the Burmese Cat from her bed beneath a small shrub (the wind was chill so she was using her pink teacosy as a sleeping-bag). 'Blow it down!'

'Piglets!' shouted the B.B.Wolf through the window of the new brick house. 'It's me – the tewwifying old Wolf again! If you do not leave immediately, I'll puff and I'll huff – no, the other way round – but anyway I'll *blow* the house down!'

Once again the piglets were far too busy with their music to see or hear the Wolf. And what was truly amazing was that their playing was getting very much better. It was now quieter and smoother and really rather enjoyable to listen to.

So the Bean Bag Wolf huffed and he puffed, and then he *blew*... but this time nothing happened. Bun's brick rehearsal room was Wolf-proof.

'I'm a failure!' moaned the B.B.Wolf. 'Always have been all my life. No good at being a Wolf. Too soft. Can't even fwighten three little piglets…'

'Pull yourself together, Wolf!' snapped the Cat. 'I know what will do the trick. Climb up on the roof, slide down the chimney and spring out of the fireplace shouting, *"Piglets Out! Piglets Out!"* as loudly as you can.'

Inside Bun's cosy, wind-proof rehearsal room, things were going very well indeed. The piglets' sad pop song was now very good. The guitars were melancholy and Bun had calmed down her drumming so that it was just a rhythmic beat behind the guitars. 'You know what we desperately need now,' Bun said suddenly. 'A singer! Our sad song has got to be *sung*, not just played.'

AAAAARRRGHOOOH

Hot and Cross knew she was right. But neither of them could sing a note in tune, let alone the sort of pop song which needed a deep, tragic voice. Sad singers are hard to find.

At that moment the B.B.Wolf was having a bad time in the chimney. It was a modern chimney and narrow. The other animals had helped to squeeze him head first down the chimney-pot and now, whimpering with fear, the Wolf was trying to wriggle his way downwards. But after a couple of painful wriggles he found himself stuck fast. Terrified of the dark, he panicked.

'Aaaaaghoooooooh!' he howled. 'Eeeeeoooooouuuarrrrrr! Yeewoo - yooweee - AHHHHHHH!'

Down below, Bun pricked up her ears. *'That voice!'* she cried. 'That mournful howl of misery! *That's our sad singer!'*

The three little pigs rushed up to the roof and plucked the Wolf out of the chimney like a cork out of a bottle. They scrubbed him clean, sat him down and gave him their song to learn.

As everybody knows, the song was recorded the following day (a Tuesday) by the piglets and the B.B.Wolf. It sold millions in a week and very soon became Number 1, Top of the Pops throughout the civilized world.

The gentle Wolf, a failure as a wolf, became a much loved and rich Pop Star. And so did Hot, Cross and Bun, who bought their mother a commodious house in the superior part of the New Forest.

Thus ends happily the true story of the birth of the fabbest pop group of all time:

Bean Bag Wolfy and the Pork Scratchings.

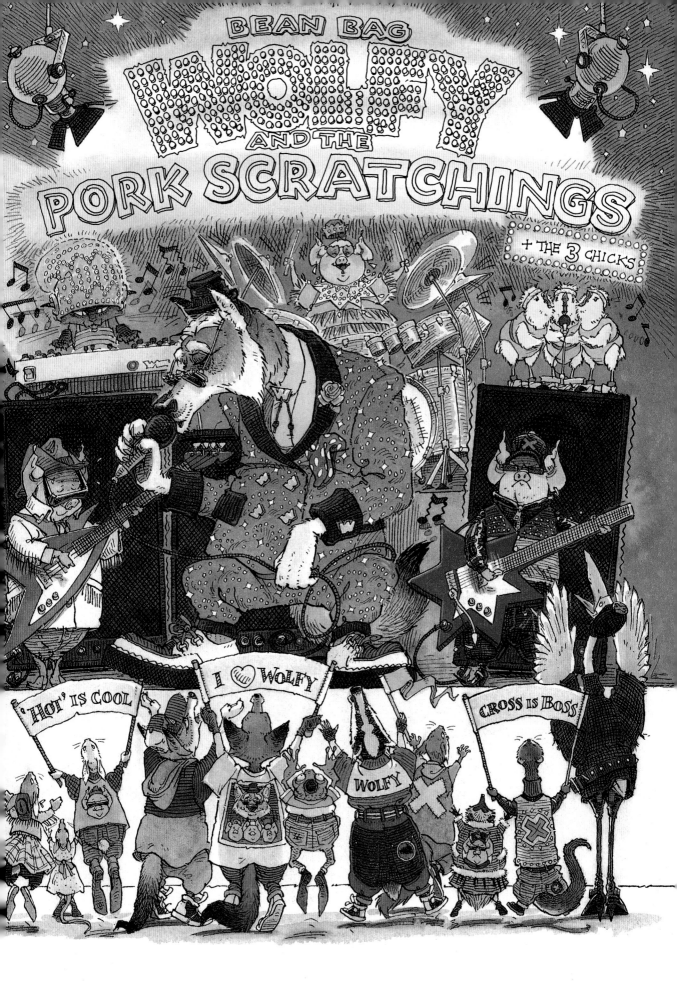